Visit us on the web at www.clavisbooks.com

Baba Yaga written and illustrated by An Leysen
Original title: *Baba Jaga*
Translated from the Dutch by Clavis Publishing

ISBN 978-1-60537-290-7

This book was printed in April 2016 at Publikum d.o.o., Slavka Rodica 6, Belgrade, Serbia

First Edition
10 9 8 7 6 5 4 3 2 1

Clavis Publishing supports the First Amendment and celebrates the right to read

BABA YAGA
An Leysen
Clavis
NEW YORK

BABA YAGA

is an ugly old witch.
She has a rusty witches' cauldron
that flies by itself,
while Baba Yaga paddles and steers
with all her might
using a wooden oar
and a broom to hide her tracks
in the cold, dark night.

Stranger still is her house,
all crooked and bent.
It runs around on chicken legs!
And sometimes, it turns around and around,
as if it's dancing.

Baba Yaga's face is covered with warts,
and she likes nasty old toads.
Her long brown fingernails make her hands look like claws
and in her mouth she has just two teeth,
rotten but razor-sharp.

And you should know this:
they say that she uses them…
to eat naughty children!

A LONG, LONG TIME AGO, in a land far away, lived a rich widow and his only daughter, Olga. They were happy together, just the two of them. There was plenty of everything: their table was always full of food and their house was always filled with laughter.

In the summer, Olga and her father played catch-me-if-you-can or hide-and-seek in the garden. Or they lay stretched out on the grass, staring dreamily at the clouds drifting by. In the winter, when it was storming outside or the world was covered with a white carpet of snow, they sat together by the fire and told stories about brave knights and clever princesses.

It was a happy time.

Olga's mother suddenly fell ill and died when her daughter was still very young. Just before she died, she gave Olga a very special doll. The doll was made out of wood and beautifully painted. Her eyes were so real that it looked as if she was looking at you. Her rosy cheeks were covered with freckles, just like Olga's. **"Keep this doll close to you and always take good care of her,"** Olga's mother had told her. "She will protect you when I'm no longer around." From that moment on, Olga always carried the doll with her, hidden in the deep pockets of her apron.

ONE DAY Olga's father fell in love again. The woman looked nice and smiled like a lady, but Olga didn't really trust her. It seemed as if she was hiding a dark secret behind that big smile. Of course, Olga knew that the beautiful lady's sister was Baba Yaga, a hideous old crone who lived alone in the dark forest. Olga had heard that Baba Yaga had magical powers and hunted the starry skies at night in her flying cauldron, while her blood-curdling laugh chilled you to the bone. People said Baba Yaga was a ***WITCH***, and that children had better stay away from her. Because, according to the stories, Baba Yaga loved little children… especially their sweet, tender flesh!

Olga's father had never heard of Baba Yaga. He was blinded by love, and pretty soon the happy couple decided to marry. Now Olga had a stepmother.

From that moment on, everything changed.

No more games or stories by the fire. And worst of all: the house was no longer filled with laughter. Olga couldn't even sit at the table when dinner was being served. Her stepmother kept all the good food for herself and threw an old crust of bread at Olga. "Find a place to eat outside!" she then barked. She told her husband that Olga was spoiled and that she needed to learn some manners. Olga's father, who seemed to be under some kind of spell, believed her. And so the poor little girl ate dry bread in the garden all by herself.
Olga had barely eaten her last bite when her stepmother called her back inside to wash the dirty dishes, make up the beds, clean the windows, sweep the floors, do the laundry and polish the shoes.
Every day it was the same. And every day Olga cleaned without complaining. Indeed, the girl was always kind and cheerful. And that made her stepmother ***FURIOUS.***
She couldn't stand having Olga around the house for a minute longer.

Olga's stepmother came up with a clever plan to get rid of Olga once and for all. When her husband left for work early in the morning, she called for her stepdaughter. "Go to your aunt, my dear sister. She lives deep in the woods. Ask her for a needle and thread to sew a new shirt for your father."

"But we have needles and thread right here," the girl said, her voice shaking. She'd heard the stories about her step-aunt.

"Be quiet," her stepmother snapped. "Do as you're told or elsssse I'll tell your father you've been a bad girl…."

She gnashed her teeth so loudly that it made Olga shudder.

"H-How do I find her?"

THE STEPMOTHER pinched Olga's nose so hard that she had tears in her eyes. "Do you feel this? This is your nose! Well, follow it from the village to the woods and then keep going until you hear nothing but the sound of creaking branches and the gurgling of the stream. Then you'll see an old wall. Climb over the wall and follow your nose until you see your aunt's little house. And believe me," she said with a nasty grin, **"you'll know it when you see it!"**

OLGA didn't know whom she ought to fear most: Baba Yaga or her stepmother. She reached into the deep pocket of her apron for the doll her mother had given her, and she begged, sobbing: "Dear doll, you HAVE to help me! My stepmother wants me to go to Baba Yaga for a needle and thread, but I'm so scared that mean witch will eat me!"

To Olga's surprise, the doll suddenly answered: **"Of course you're afraid!** No child that ever went near her was ever seen again. But if you do as I say, you can trick her. You have to find some meat, a handkerchief and some cheese before you leave."

Right away, Olga ran into the kitchen, where she found some cheese and a few gnawed-off chicken legs. She put everything inside a big handkerchief, tied a firm knot and ran out the door. Towards the woods.

AT THE END of the big road, a small path wound into the dark forest. Olga followed the path for hours, until the only things she could hear were the branches crackling under her feet and the murmur of the stream. She reached a crumbling wall and climbed over. Far away, in a clearing in the woods, she saw her aunt's house. Her mouth fell open in surprise.

BABA YAGA'S HOUSE looked like nothing Olga had ever seen before. It wasn't welcoming at all! And you couldn't call it pretty either, with its weather-beaten walls and warped window frames.

But strangest of all was this: the house was walking around on tall, scaly chicken legs! Olga carefully crept closer. The house on chicken legs turned around with the front door facing her, as if it was expecting her. Then Olga suddenly heard loud sobbing.

Baba Yaga's maid was standing in front of the house, crying her heart out. Olga forgot her fears and walked towards her. "What's the matter? Why are you crying?"

"Oh, little girl," the maid snuffled, "that mean witch gives me so much to do. My work never ends and then she gets so mad; she beats me black and blue." She tried to wipe away her tears with her skirt, but it was already soaked. Olga took the bundle with the cheese and chicken bones. She emptied the handkerchief into the pockets of her apron, shook out the crumbs and handed it to the maid. The maid gratefully took the handkerchief and smiled at Olga through her tears.

“**Baba Yaga is inside,**” the maid said softly.
“I believe she is waiting for you.”
Olga gathered her courage and knocked on the door.
It opened very slowly, its hinges creaking.

INSIDE, it was even colder and darker than in the woods,
and it took a while for Olga’s eyes to adjust to the darkness.
And there sat Baba Yaga spinning, hidden away in a corner.
She was so ***UGLY!***
And so old! Surely more than a hundred years old.
Her face was all wrinkled and covered in warts.
Her bent and bony fingers had long brown nails, just like claws!
On her head was a disgusting, green toad that gave Olga
a threatening look.

WHEN BABA YAGA noticed the girl, she stopped spinning at once. She narrowed her eyes and stretched out her wrinkled neck. Further and further it stretched, so she could get a closer look at Olga. “Come on in, my dear niece!” she said with a croaking voice. “How sweet of you to come and visit your old aunt.”

“M-m-my stepmother sent m-me to get a n-needle and thread,” Olga stammered.

“Oh, did she now?” the witch said with a false laugh, because she knew all too well how much her sister hated the little girl. “No hurry! I will find you a needle and thread. In the meantime I will run you a nice, warm bath, so you can rest from your long journey.”

Baba Yaga called the maid and ordered her in a commanding voice: **“Fill a bath for my little niece!”**

And in a whisper, so Olga couldn’t hear her, she added: “Make sure the water is boiling hot, and scrub her all soft and clean. I’m going to take a nap and when I wake up I’m going to make a nice meal out of her!”

The maid brought in a big pile of wood to make a fire and started to drag buckets of water to fill the bath.

"**Careful!**" the doll in Olga's apron warned her. "This isn't just a bath! Your aunt wants to cook you in boiling hot water until you're tender enough to eat! Tell the maid she doesn't have to hurry making the fire and tell her not to use a bucket to fill the tub, but a sieve with holes in it." Olga did what the doll told her to do. The maid, who still remembered Olga's kindness, didn't say a word but only winked knowingly.
Then she worked really slowly at making the fire.

While the maid was busy preparing the bath, no one kept an eye on Olga.
The girl sneaked to the door on her tiptoes. Careful,
don't make a sound.... ***Shhhhh!***

But before Olga could reach the doorknob...

… a huge cat

JUMPED

in front of her.

“Get out of my way!” the cat shouted. “Can’t you see I’m trying to catch a mouse? ***Meooooow!*** I haven’t eaten anything for three days! And now my dinner has escaped!” She gave Olga an angry look and arched her back. Then she stuck out her sharp claws one by one.

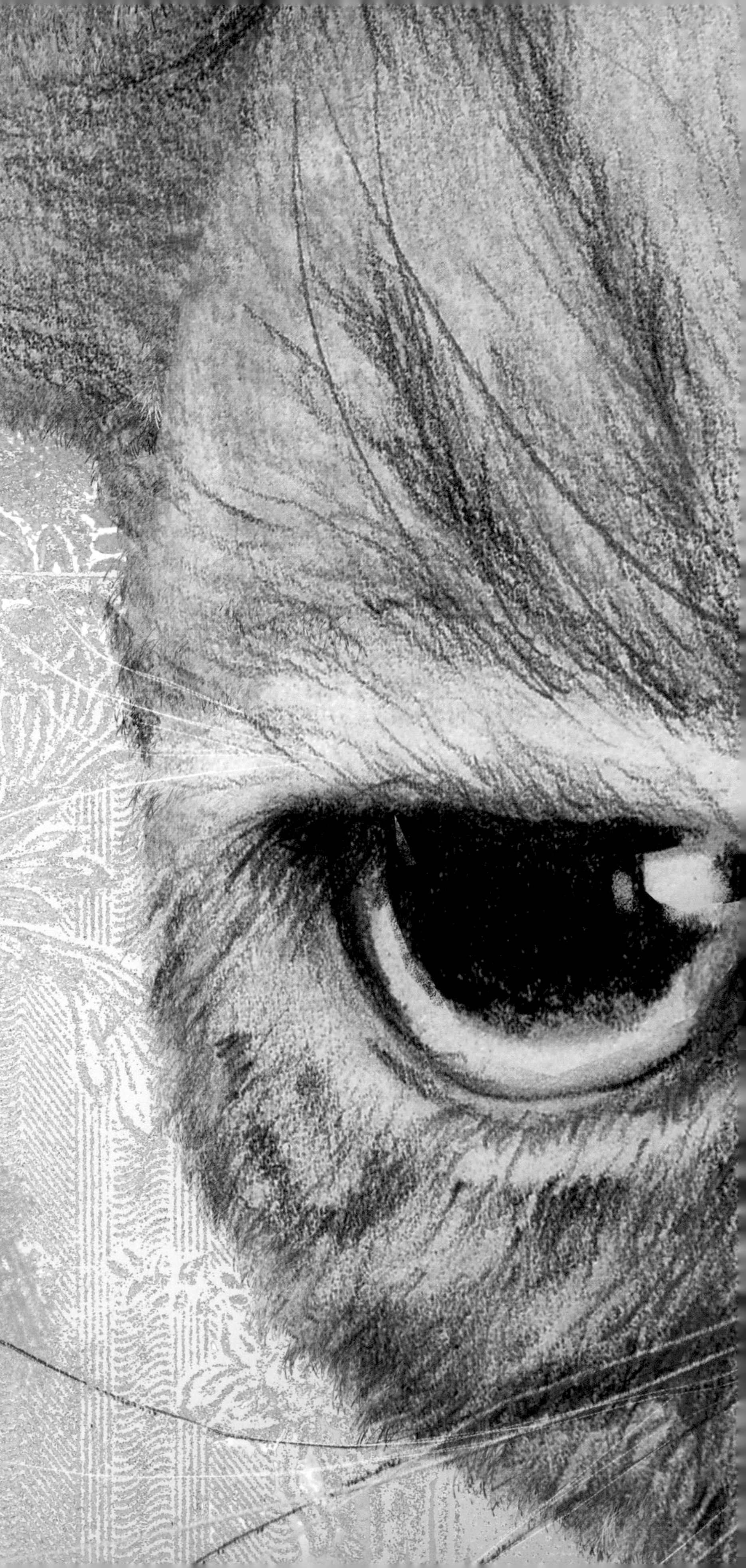

LUCKILY Olga remembered the cheese in her pocket. She threw the cheese to the cat, who ate it greedily. "Mmm," the animal smacked its lips. **"That was delicious."** She started to purr loudly. The cat looked far less dangerous and Olga carefully petted her back. "Oh, sweet cat, I'm so scared Baba Yaga will eat me.... Can you help me?" The cat took her time washing her whiskers before she answered: "Hmm... yes, that's what she's planning to do. But I know a way for you to escape! There is a comb and a towel on the chair. Take them both and run as fast as your legs can carry you. Baba Yaga will soon catch up with you in her cauldron! But if you're smart, the comb and the towel can help you. Good luck, little girl."

OLGA followed the cat's advice and grabbed the wooden comb and the towel. Before she ran off, she wanted to make sure the witch was really asleep. But when she peeked into the other room, she looked straight into the eyes of a huge, growling dog. **Olga shrank in fear.**

THE DOG crept closer, ready to attack Olga.
Luckily the doll saved her just in time: "Give him the meat!" she called.
The girl threw the chicken legs and the dog hungrily caught them in the air.
He lay down with his head on his paws and started eating.
Olga didn't hesitate and started running. She was far away from the house
when Baba Yaga woke up from her afternoon nap.

THE WITCH, who awoke very hungry and was looking forward to a tasty meal,
hurried to the bathroom to see if her niece was ready to be eaten.
But to her dismay, the bathtub was empty. She realized that Olga had escaped
and quickly ran outside. **"Come back, my dear little niece,"**
she called in her sweetest voice, **"you forgot your needle and thread!"**
When no one answered, she turned around and stormed back into the house.
There she saw the dog gnawing on the chicken bones.

"YOU!" Baba Yaga roared. "You were supposed to guard my delicious meal! Why did you let her get away?"
The dog growled: "I kept guard for years and years and the only thing I got in return was old, moldy bread. That sweet little girl gave me these tasty chicken legs."
"And you?" Baba Yaga called to the cat. "Why didn't you come and warn me?"
The cat put her tail in the air and arched her back. ***"Meoooooow!"*** she snarled. "Even though I've always chased away rats and mice, I had to catch my own dinner as a thank you. But the girl gave me some delicious cheese."

Baba Yaga grabbed the cat and shook her ROUGHLY. Then she stomped off to the maid, who was still busy carrying water to the bath with a sieve.
"Lazy maid, why is it taking so long for you to fill the bath?"
The maid was shaking. "Oh, Baba Yaga, I've always served you well. I was always good and did my work without complaining. Never was I rewarded, except maybe with a beating. But the little girl gave me a beautiful handkerchief to dry my tears."
Baba Yaga started yelling and screaming: **"Good-for-nothings!** Wait until I come back, then I'll make you pay!" There's no way she could know that the maid, the dog and the cat would run off together as soon as she'd left the house.

Then Baba Yaga snapped her fingers and the flying cauldron flew to her. She climbed in and gave a loud tap with her oar. "Let's go! I'm hungry!"

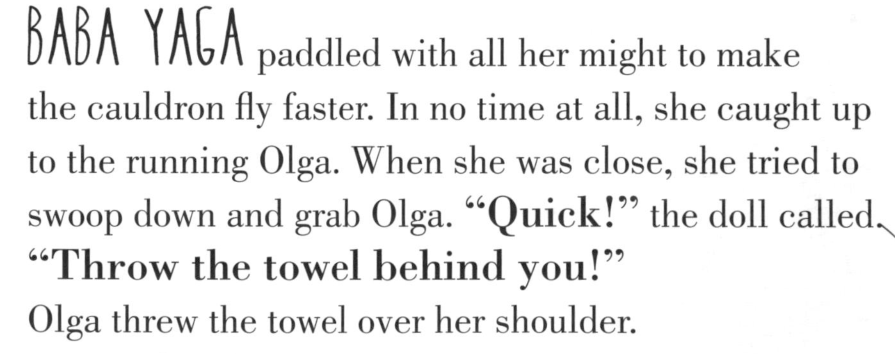

BABA YAGA paddled with all her might to make the cauldron fly faster. In no time at all, she caught up to the running Olga. When she was close, she tried to swoop down and grab Olga. **"Quick!"** the doll called. **"Throw the towel behind you!"**
Olga threw the towel over her shoulder.
It immediately grew larger and changed into a deep, wide river.

BABA YAGA let out a horrifying scream. She was scared to death of water! Furious, she flew back to her house to get her only cow. The poor animal hadn't had any food or water for weeks.

"Drink! Drink!" the witch shrieked.
The cow, happy that she could fill her belly,
drank the whole river, to the last drop.
Baba Yaga jumped back into her cauldron
and flew over the dry river.

IN THE MEANTIME, Olga had gotten a head start and hoped she was rid of the witch for good. But to her dismay she saw a dark shadow approaching in the distance. Then she remembered **the comb!** That could stop the witch! With a wave of her arm she threw it in the direction of the flying cauldron.

The comb had barely hit the ground when the teeth began to grow longer and longer. They grew into giant trees! In a few seconds there was a thick, dark forest between Olga and Baba Yaga.

The witch tried to fly through, but the cauldron was too big and too unwieldy and the witch got caught in the branches.

"OLGAAAAAAA!

Olga, my dearest niece, come back!" she called.

"Your stepmother will be very angry when you come home without needle and thread!"

Olga ignored the shrieking and didn't look back. She hurried through the woods, down the path, faster and faster. There was her father, waiting for her. Exhausted but happy, Olga fell into his arms.

SUDDENLY Olga's stepmother came outside too.
When she saw the girl, she went all red and then purple with anger.
She gnashed her teeth so hard that they all fell out. Her plan had failed!
Impossible! Her sister had let Olga get away!
Olga's father was just as furious, no longer blinded by love.
He raged and thundered and drove the mean stepmother into the woods.

NOW OLGA and her father were alone again, just the two of them. Laughter was heard in the house once again, and they played games together and told each other exciting stories by the fire. And soon this whole adventure was nothing but a bad memory.

And the stepmother?
No one ever saw her again.
(Who knows, maybe there are two witches in the house on chicken legs now?)

The end